THE THIRST OF A LOVING TRUNK

WRITTEN BY TRAVIS CHING
ILLUSTRATED BY SHAY ALLRED

Edited by Vince Font
Original artwork by Shay Allred
Published by Glass Spider Publishing
www.glassspiderpublishing.com

"The biggest change will be in the children," said the little voice.
(11/20/2018)

We dedicate this book to all the loving grandparents, mothers,
fathers, and children of our beautiful world.
We love and thank you all for supporting us on our journey of
creating this wonderful classic.

TO: _____

FROM: _____

The wind sang as dust storms danced across the plains of Africa.

"Mom, how much longer until we find water? I am starting to get thirsty," said Atheena.

Leading the herd with confidence, a wise Mother spoke, "Don't worry, Atheena! We still have a ways to go. Focus on your steps, and they will add up to miles. Before you know it, you will be playing and drinking water all day."

Atheena loved the thought of playing.

"That sounds wonderful, Mom! I can't wait to play! Grandma, do you want to play with me first?"

Grandma's loving trunk tickled Atheena's ear.

"I would love to! We will splash and play for days!"

Atheena filled up her sneaky little trunk with an idea.

"We will splash like this, right, Grandma?" she yelled out.

A small cloud of dust filled the air as if it were water.

Grandma's trunk instantly filled the air with more.

"It's going to be better than you can imagine, Atheena. I promise!"

Loving memories flowed into an old mind. Memories of playing with the one she loved, the one she still missed, the one she herself had once called Grandma.

Dust tickled their faces as it fell back to earth.

With the burn of the afternoon sun, it looked like there was water all around.

"Mom!" Atheena yelled out with excitement. "Over there! Isn't that water? Grandma, I found water!"

Mother's smile was all Atheena noticed as she was shielded from the heat of the day.

"No, baby girl, that's a tricky mirage. If that were water, your trunk would have smelled it from miles away. When I was your age, I asked Grandma the same question."

Atheena looked up as Grandma's trunk blew cool air onto her head and down her body. "She sure did. Wow, Atheena! I can't believe how much you look like your mother."

As the day was coming to an end, an important question popped into Atheena's mind.

"Mom," she asked, "why am I the only baby elephant in our group?"

Looking down into innocent eyes, Mother answered.

"Atheena, that is a wonderful question! During the drier years, only the strong-willed are born, and baby girl, we all know that is you. Let me ask you a question. Do you love this day?"

Atheena smiled. "I do love this day! You taught me to smell with my trunk first and let my brain decide if it's water or another tricky mirage! And Mom, we are one day closer to me drinking and splashing with Grandma!"

She skipped along, happy with her answers.

"Wow, Athena, I can't wait to hear your answers when the rains come and make life easy," Mother said. "Guess what else you're closer to?"

Atheena's little excited ears opened wide to catch the answer. "Mom, what am I closer to? Please tell me!"

Proud, Mother stopped the herd for this special moment. "To achieve your purpose in life. To someday lead and protect our loving herd. My responsibility is to teach you the wisdom I've learned from Grandma, and together we will learn new ways to lead."

Atheena's trunk rested on her mother's. "I get it, Mom. You are teaching me where to lead the herd during the dry times, so when the rainy times come it will be even better, right?"

Atheena's answers pleased everyone who could hear.

"You're right, Atheena. I promise I will get us there! It's just a bit farther."

Out of the darkness, a fire danced into view.

The smell of smoke opened Atheena's eyes to excitement moving all around.

"Mom, what's going on? What is that brightness? Why is everyone so scared?"

Mother's voice lined up the herd.

"Atheena, you don't have to worry. Please get up and grab onto my tail."

Atheena stood up, wanting to know everything about this beautiful brightness that shined over the land.

Her heart and mind began to race faster and faster with excitement, not even noticing her trunk was squeezing tighter and tighter.

"Relax your trunk, baby girl, and breathe," Mother said. "Look at me. You're right about the other animals. They are scared because at one point in their lives, the fire has taken someone they loved."

Then Mother asked, "Do you want to hear my favorite story?"

Atheena loved stories. "Yes, Mom. Please tell me!" she said, tugging gently on her mother's tail.

"When I was young, Atheena, I witnessed my hero save everyone! Can you guess who it was?"

Atheena shook her head, not knowing any heroes—or so she thought. "My hero is Grandma." Excited goosebumps stood up on Atheena's skin. She wanted to know more about the hero she loved.

"It all started with a strong wind that brought a fire into our valley! Everyone panicked like today, except Grandma! Her first instinct was to run, knowing if she did, some of us would be left behind. One of them would have been me. Our faith in Grandma kept everyone calm while she searched for a solution."

"Look up there," Mother said. "See how the wind controls the direction of the fire?"

Atheena nodded.

"I will never forget how relieved and thankful we all felt when she saw that and led us all to safety. Because of Grandma, I'm leading you to safety."

Atheena's mind absorbed all of the wisdom being shared. "What a great story, Mom! Thanks, Grandma, for teaching Mom about the not so scary fire! You both are my heroes!"

Tears ran down an older cheek, thankful she had raised such a confident and loving daughter to become a better version of herself.

Grandma tickled Atheena's back, and the cutest scream of joy came out as they all started to move.

The fire was blazing closer and closer.

Atheena saw there was a commotion going on up ahead.

"Mom," she said, "those birds need our help! Their nest is in the way of the fire!"

Looking down at Atheena's pointing trunk, Mother answered, "I'm sorry, but we only take care of our kind!"

Atheena pleaded again.

"They need our help! Will anyone help?"

One by one, the elephants of the herd shook their heads as they followed their leader.

Atheena felt lost and defeated. Her eyes closed, listening to the fire cracking and popping as it danced up a tree.

"Don't worry, Atheena," whispered a small voice. "I will help you."

Atheena's eyes opened to see who would help and found no one there.

"We must first get Mother to agree," the voice continued.

Atheena slowly nodded her head up and down.

"Thank you for helping me, little voice," she whispered. "Now, what can we do?"

A breeze of loving conversation flowed into Atheena's mind and out her lips.

"Mom, please stop!" she said. "Please listen! For me to become a great leader someday, I will need to make good decisions, right?"

This simple question stopped everyone but the one she needed.

Several more steps went by before the leader turned to hear the answer. Proud disbelief rushed through her body. Atheena had already turned the herd.

"Please, Mom! Look at those babies in the nest as if they were me. What would you want some loving strangers to do?"

Atheena's loving spirit pierced everyone's minds and left no doubts as she spoke up for the ones who needed her help.

"You are right, Atheena. I would want some strangers to help. I would want them to keep you safe."

Mother's large trunk gently pulled the nest down from the tree.

"Thank you, Mom, for understanding. Can I please carry the nest?"

Meeting three of the cutest faces for the first time, Atheena said, "It's okay, you're safe now. Our herd will love and protect you. Look, Mom! The birds know we are trying to help! We must find their family the best home and be their solution like Grandma did for us."

The loving act of kindness ran through the minds of the herd.

Atheena's days found new joy in carrying the nest.

She watched them fly back and forth, never stopping until all three bellies were full.

"Mom, they are such good parents! They are both working so hard to make things work, trusting in me to help!"

Glad that Atheena could focus on something that brought her so much joy, Mother said, "You're right, baby. They are great parents! It goes to show you, all animals want what's best for their children."

Atheena's new friends distracted her from her tired legs, moving one in front of the other as the miles slowly passed.

A beautiful tree was coming into view.

"Atheena, do you want to put the bird's nest up in that tree?" asked Mother.

Atheena closed her eyes and saw water, trees, and lots of birds flying around. Her eyes opened. "No, Mom. I want to give these birds the best life and put them next to the water so their parents don't have to fly so far to find food!"

Proud of her daughter's caring answer, Mother replied, "That's a great idea. I'm going to tell you a secret."

Atheena loved secrets.

"We should be at the water by tonight!"

Atheena's mind instantly daydreamed about how much fun her first splash with Grandma was going to be, and the beautiful tree she would find for her new friends.

Atheena watched as her mother's trunk searched for water.

Disappointment and dust was all they found in the riverbed.

Mother turned and spoke only to Grandma.

"It's always been here, Mom. Why isn't the water here?"

Atheena could feel the worry in her mother's voice.

Grandma looked down with concern in her eyes that Atheena had never seen before.

"We will rest here for the night and figure out what to do in the morning," Grandma said.

That night, Atheena dreamed that she was leading the herd. A feeling of confidence grew inside of her, knowing she would not have to do it alone.

"Gather around and listen to me," Atheena said. "There is no reason to be scared. We have a friend that will help us find a solution. Please, little voice, will you help me? Please, will you help our loving herd?"

Atheena watched the birds come and go, patiently listening for a reply.

"I will always help you!" came the voice. "The key to finding water is in the birds. Follow our birds."

Atheena's voice awoke Mother. "Wake up, Mom! Everyone, wake up! I know how to find water!"

The herd turned and looked at their youngest member.

"When the birds leave their nest," Atheena said, "they fly away in the same direction every day. That means they are getting bugs for their babies around water! If we go in the direction of the birds, I promise we will find water!"

Atheena watched as everyone pondered the idea. Grandma's smile backed the leader's decision. "I believe in you, Atheena. Show us the way!"

Atheena smiled as she looked into the eyes of her birds. "My little voice said to follow you. Please, will you lead us to water?"

She pointed with the nest as the birds took flight. Many in the group wondered if Atheena's plan would find them water.

Mile after mile, the herd followed faithfully up a steep hill. Atheena looked back, proud of how far they had come. A beautiful valley greeted them at the top. Then the little voice came to visit. "Look up, Atheena. Isn't it beautiful?"

Atheena's tired eyes went from clear to blurry and back to clear. "You're right, little voice, that is a beautiful mirage. I want to thank you. Because of you, I am leading our loving herd."

A mother's kiss came into their conversation. Atheena looked up at her hero with spent legs and a beautiful smile. "Atheena," she said, "tell Mom about the little voice."

Atheena closed her eyes, remembering all the loving guidance she had received. "Mom, the little voice is a loving friend that has been with us since we helped our birds. The little voice helps me make the best decisions. The little voice is a hero!"

Atheena's trunk pointed into the distance. "Mom! Grandma! Look over there! Isn't that the most beautiful mirage you've ever seen?"

Her legs wobbled. Grandma's trunk locked underneath with Mom's. Both kept Atheena from falling to the ground.

Everyone came to a stop. Could it be? Their hearts raced, not believing what they could smell and now see in the distance.

"Atheena, look again. What's different about this mirage?" asked Mother.

The herd stood in silence, knowing how hard Atheena had pushed herself to this special moment. The wind swirled, bringing the smell of water up Atheena's trunk.

"Water, Mom! I smell water! Everyone, we have made it! We are finally here!" Atheena's body filled with new hope.

There were animals all around enjoying the waterhole. Atheena looked one last time before handing the nest to her mother. Everyone was flooded with joy. Feelings of peace ran through their minds knowing faith in Atheena had gotten them here.

"You did it!" said Mother. "You saved the herd! You are a hero!"

Everyone's trunks cheered as Atheena splashed in toward Grandma. Atheena felt her strength returning as she drank the cool water, knowing she had not done it alone.

"Mom, this will be a beautiful story that my daughters will tell someday about a loving little voice that helped guide a little girl to water, teaching our loving herd that there is always a solution found by helping others. Mom, that tree will be perfect for our heroes' new home!"

To all who are reading, and you know who you are, when you find someone in need, you can be their bright star. Tomorrow is coming. Please be prepared, for the person or animal you choose to help might find you there!

Good night, Atheena.

Good night, little voice.

Good night, beautiful birds.

Good night, peaceful elephants.

Good night, little dreamers.

We love you all!

We believe in our loving purpose found first in family. How happy the children of our world could all wake up in the morning because of meaningful lessons planted into their subconscious minds.

Shay and I want to reconnect others to the importance of reading and loving one another. Please help our message grow by buying another copy or passing this book on for someone else to enjoy, young or old.

TRAVIS CHING is and always will be a dreamer of life, inspiring many and never a few, knowing happiness is found in sound relationships with family, friends, and a loving relationship with the infinite. One day, he found himself in front of a computer he didn't even know the family password to. He started writing every morning from three to six with nothing more than a little voice by his side, and that is how he became a writer. If you ever get a chance to meet him and see his handwriting, you will know what a miracle looks like.

SHAY ALLRED is not just any illustrator; he is my brother of life. A wonderful human being who is a devoted father, friend, and partner. He teaches others the patience of doing something right the first time, and he has a mind that works in total harmony with his hands. He is a true craftsman and builder of anything.

Made in the USA
Monee, IL
01 November 2020